MOLLY&MAE

To all in the L & T family, and the journeys yet to come—D.P.

To my childhood friend Sally Hardy—F.B.

Text copyright © 2016 by Danny Parker
Illustrations copyright © 2016 by Freya Blackwood
First published in Australia by Little Hare, an imprint of Hardie Grant Egmont, in 2016.
First published in the United States by Houghton Mifflin Harcourt in 2017.

www.hmhco.com

Library of Congress Cataloging-in-Publication Data is available.
ISBN 978-1-328-71543-2

Manufactured in China
10 9 8 7 6 5 4 3 2 1
PO 4500640637

LITTLE HARE

OLLY & MAE

Written by **DANNY PARKER**   Illustrated by **FREYA BLACKWOOD**

HOUGHTON MIFFLIN HARCOURT

Boston   New York

PLATFORM

Molly found Mae
beneath a bench.

Mae found Molly
in the newspaper shop.

Molly's mom found them
blowing bubbles together.

After that, Molly and Mae were stuck.

TIMETABLE

At 8:24, photographs.

At 8:32, balancing.

At 8:40, ballet.

At 8:45, sherbet.

At 9:05, secrets.

At 9:10, forever.

All aboard!

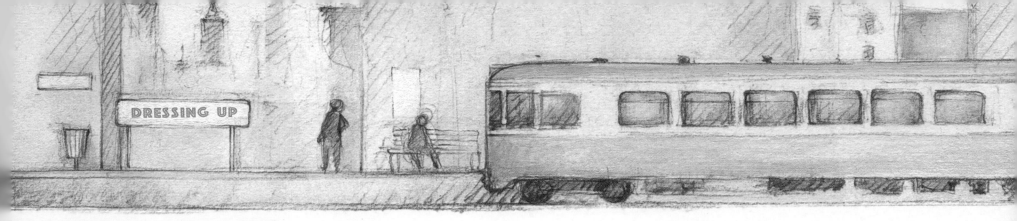

DRESSING UP

JOURNEY →

Next, dressing up dolls . . .   waiting and getting hungry . . .

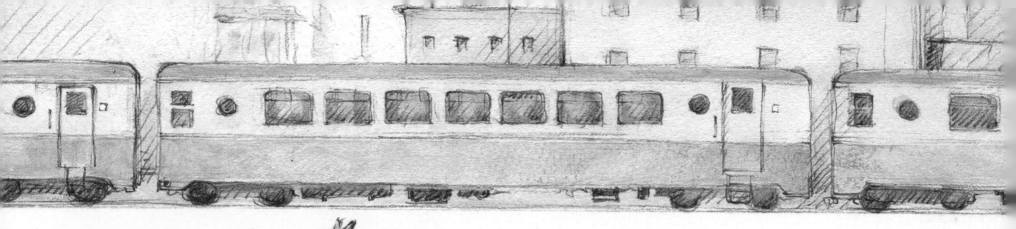

jumping and bouncing and
hanging upside down . . .

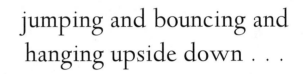

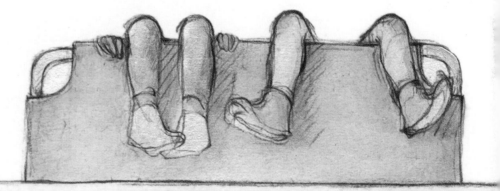

annoying Molly's mom . . .   annoying others . . .

being quiet and sitting still.

Then on to I Spy:
Something beginning with *F*.

But then . . .
Molly thought Mae was silly and told her so.
Mae was tired of being bossed around.

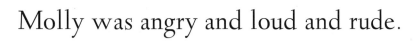

Molly was angry and loud and rude.

Molly turned her back.

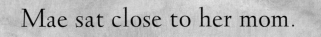

Mae sat close to her mom.

FROM THE WINDOW

The rain made the outside smeary,
made fields and farms dull.

The whole world looked murky.

Drawing on the glass,
Molly and Mae missed each other.

So Molly took the words
she shouldn't have said
and hid them.

Then she took the words
she should have said
and started
to build a bridge.

Mae added some words of her own . . .

until the bridge was strong enough
to hold them both.

TRACKS

The journey stretched
as far as they could see
in both directions.

There were hills and valleys,
bends and straight runs,
bridges and tunnels.

And the train traveled on.

DESTINATION

Molly and Mae helped
each other pack up.
Everything fit neatly.

Then, holding hands,
they jumped out
together.